WOL

Cumbria
County Council

Libraries, books and more...........

Please return/renew this item by the last date shown.
Library items may also be renewed by phone on
030 33 33 1234 (24hours) or via our website

www.cumbria.gov.uk/libraries

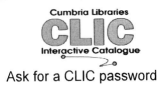

Cumbria Libraries

CLIC
Interactive Catalogue

Ask for a CLIC password

Special thanks to Michael Ford

To Theodore

ORCHARD BOOKS

First published in Great Britain in 2018 by The Watts Publishing Group

1 3 5 7 9 10 8 6 4 2

Text © 2018 Beast Quest Limited
Cover and inside illustrations by Dynamo
© Beast Quest Limited 2018

Team Hero is a registered trademark in the European Union
Series created by Beast Quest Limited, London

A CIP catalogue record for this book is available from the British Library.

ISBN 978 1 40835 207 6

Printed in Great Britain

The paper and board used in this book are made from wood from responsible sources.

Orchard Books
An imprint of Hachette Children's Group
Part of The Watts Publishing Group Limited
Carmelite House, 50 Victoria Embankment, London EC4Y 0DZ

An Hachette UK Company
www.hachette.co.uk
www.hachettechildrens.co.uk

THE SHADOW
STALLION

ADAM BLADE

ORCHARD

MEET TEAM HERO ...

JACK

POWER: Super-strength

LIKES: Ventura City FC

DISLIKES: Bullies

RUBY

POWER: Fire vision

LIKES: Comic books

DISLIKES: Small spaces

DANNY

POWER: Super-hearing, able to generate sonic blasts

LIKES: Pizza

DISLIKES: Thunder

CONTENTS

OLLY STRAINED against the metal manacles on his wrists and ankles until beads of sweat broke out across his forehead. The Legionaries might be weaklings, but they had made sure he was securely fastened. They'd even tried to remove the Flameguard, though the fools had failed. The scaled armour was fused to his body. It was part of him now.

Spreadeagled on the wall, Olly stared in anger at the closed cell door opposite.

"How dare they do this to me?" he growled.

His heart thumped furiously against the breastplate, but he told himself to be calm. Better to bide his time, for now. And when he did find a way out ...

"I'll have my revenge on them all — Heroes and Legionaries alike."

He licked his dry lips at the thought of raining down fire upon his enemies. Of course, there'd be no quick death for Jack and his friends. They might have bested him once through sheer luck, but the next time they met, things would be different. They'd feel his true power, and they would *beg* for mercy.

Olly's burning anger kept him plotting ways to get revenge on his enemies, but deep down he also felt a spark of concern. Since the day he'd first put on the magical breastplate, he'd heard Raina's voice in his head. Comforting. Commanding. Powerful. But since his capture, there had been only silence. It was as if she had abandoned him, and that hurt a lot

more than the metal bonds biting
into his limbs. Olly let his head sag
for a moment.

*If she's deserted me, what does that
mean?* he thought.

"I have not deserted you, young
one," said a voice.

Olly's head jerked up. Standing
inside the door was a slight figure
wearing a dark cloak and deep hood.
Its edges blurred and shifted, as if
cast in firelight.

"Raina!" he gasped.

She lifted a hand in front of her
face, extending a long bony finger
with filthy, cracked nails. "Quiet, my

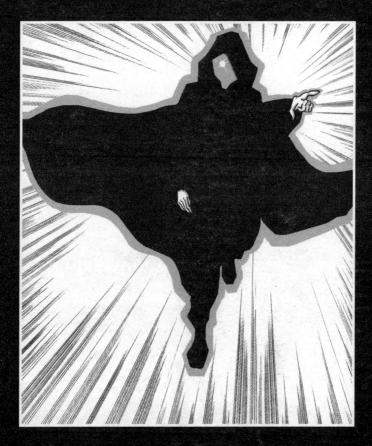

loyal servant. We do not have long."

"Get me out of here!" said Olly,
struggling against the metal.

Raina drifted forwards, and pointed towards his chest. Olly saw the red tendrils engraved into the Flameguard glow brighter, pulsing like bloodflow through veins. At the same time, the panic in his heart seemed to calm.

"I came here only to thank you," said Raina. "Your bravery secured for me one of the Orbs of Foresight. Now I see the way forward."

"'But you will need my help!" said Olly. "Have you come to set me free?"

Raina shook her head. "I do not have the strength yet ... but soon."

"How soon?" pushed Olly.

Raina moved away again, gliding

across the floor while still facing him.

"When it is time," she said, melting into the shadows. "And then, my servant, we will set this world ablaze."

CHAPTER 1

THE JOUST

JACK TRIED to lead the accifax by its reins, but the creature tossed her giant feathered head and let out an angry squawk.

"Easy, Flinta!" said Jack, backing off. Even though he was in full armour, he didn't fancy his chances against a hooked beak that was longer than his arm.

Some of the Legionaries assembled in the tiered stands of the jousting hall laughed, and Jack felt his cheeks burn inside his helmet. *They still think the students of Team Hero are no match for those of Mount Razor.*

"You need to be more assertive," said Captain Jana. "An accifax won't respect you unless you seem in control."

Jack looked towards the Legionary Captain standing with Danny and Ruby, wearing her dark sunglasses. Though she was blind, Jack knew her fighting senses were battle-honed like those of all the teachers here at Mount Razor. None of the students here had special powers like those at Hero Academy, but they prided themselves on being a well-drilled army nonetheless. The school had been here as long as the Academy, hidden in the Shardmaw Mountains, away from the rest of the world.

Jack turned back to the huge steed in front of him. Until recently, he'd never have believed such a creature could exist. Flinta had the body of a mountain lion, covered in coarse fur, with claws the size of daggers. But at the accifax's neck, the fur gave way to tawny feathers, and the creature's head was that of an eagle, with large black eyes. Flinta had been easy to handle for the first few rounds of the tournament, but as the day wore on, her mood had become worse.

"Go on, Jack!" said Ruby. "We know you can do it."

"Show it who's boss," said Danny.

"*It* is a *she*," Jana reminded them.

Jack gripped the reins again, and slipped a foot into the stirrup. He felt Flinta buck a little, but used the power in his glowing golden hands to hold on, then hoisted himself into the worn leather saddle.

"A promising start, Hero," said a voice. Matthias bounded past on his own accifax, armour clanking, before turning to call out again. "I wouldn't get too comfy up there, though."

Jack watched the young Legionary canter to the end of the jousting lists, where he seized a lance from a rack. The Hightower Legion shunned the tech of the modern world. The school looked like something from medieval times, with battlements and courtyards and old-fashioned weapons. The vaulted hall they were in had tapestries hanging from the stone walls, and torches blazing in sconces at regular intervals.

Captain Jana brought Jack his lance and a battered rectangular shield. Jack hooked an arm through the handles then gripped the reins again, and hefted the lance easily in his other hand. He squeezed his knees, and Flinta jerked into motion, springing nimbly to the opposite end of the jousting ground. The crowd began to clap and roar Matthias's name. Jack could see Danny and Ruby cheering him on, but their voices were well and truly drowned out. Both of Jack's friends had been knocked out of the tournament earlier by the more experienced jousters of the Legion. Jack thought perhaps he'd been lucky winning all his rounds so far, even though Jana said he was a natural.

When he was in position, the Captain raised her arm for silence, and the crowd obeyed.

"Welcome, all, to the final joust of the Founder's Day competition!" cried Captain Jana. "The mighty Wulfstan Hightower is looking on in spirit, so make him proud. Matthias and Jack, are you ready?"

Jack nodded and slid down his visor. The world was reduced to its narrow opening, and he fixed his stare on his opponent.

"Engage!" shouted Captain Jana.

Jack leant forward and squeezed his knees, driving Flinta into a trot that quickly became a bounding gallop. He watched Matthias charging from the other direction, picking up speed as well. Jack tried to stay calm, as Jana had taught him, focusing his gaze on the point of his lance. The key was not to have any doubts — to charge headlong even though your mind told you it was a *bad, bad* idea. Along the lists, the crowd were just a blur, their roaring voices indistinct. Jack gripped the lance tight, keeping it steady as they closed.

He saw the tip of Matthias's lance come at him, and angled his shield. The point slid past, then ...

SMASH!

The force almost lifted Jack from the saddle, but he held the reins firm.

And then Flinta was slowing and the world and its sounds came back into focus. Apart from his own breathing, the entire hall was silent. Everyone's faces were aghast.

Jack brought Flinta round and saw why. Matthias's accifax was riderless,

and the Legionary himself was on the ground, rolling on to his knees and shaking his head.

I did it, thought Jack. *I won!*

He slipped from the saddle, and rushed towards Matthias to check if he was OK. Before he reached him, the Legionary stood up, tugged off his helmet and tossed it aside in disgust. Jack skidded to a stop, ducking as the helmet shot over his head. "Hey!" he cried.

Matthias glared at Jack, and for a moment Jack feared he might actually lash out. But Captain Jana stepped between them and she was accompanied by Commandant Eckles, head of Mount Razor School. She was holding a silver baton. "Congratulations to Jack of Team Hero. You are this year's champion." She held out the baton to him, horizontally, then pressed a small button in the underside. It extended in a smooth motion, becoming a double-pointed spear. Along its shaft were runic engravings. Jack took it, surprised how light it felt, and nodded gratefully. He saw Danny giving him a double thumbs-up.

"It was a fluke," said Jack.

"Those super hands of his give him extra strength, remember?" grumbled Matthias.

Commandant Eckles shot him a disapproving glance. "Don't forget, Matthias, that Wulfstan Hightower himself, founder of our Legion, shared the same power." She raised her voice to address the crowd too. "And may I remind you all that our guests from Hero Academy were the ones who saved one of the Orbs of Foresight from Raina's agent, just as Wulfstan once defeated our old enemy." She pointed towards the largest of the tapestries, which showed an armour-clad warrior with the silver spear fighting against a half-dragon, half-woman riding a monstrous horse-like creature made of black smoke. Jack shuddered. When he'd touched the Orb of Foresight, he'd seen that very battle in a terrifying vision.

He just wished he'd managed to

save *both* of the Orbs. Legends told that Wulfstan had stripped Raina of her evil powers, but somehow she was back, and eager to restore them. Jack feared that the Orb of Foresight she'd recovered was just the start.

Commandant Eckles dismissed the rest of the students, who began to drift away to their lessons. Jack watched them go with deep unease. *How will they fare in a fight against Raina? I just beat their best, and I'm new at this ...*

He pushed the thought away as Matthias came up, looking sheepish.

"Listen, Jack," he said. "You beat me fair and square. I shouldn't complain."

Jack offered a friendly smile. *No one likes losing.* "It could have happened differently on another day," he said.

"Of course," said Matthias, quickly. "But we have a custom that, as the loser, I am duty bound to offer you a favour of your choice. So ask away."

Jack was taken aback, but an idea immediately leapt into his head. The Orb of

Foresight had shown him the past last time — what if it could show him the future as well?

I might discover Raina's next move.

But the Orb was kept safe under lock and key in the Legion's treasury. The treasury that Matthias and his band guarded.

"Let me touch the Orb of Foresight again," Jack said.

Matthias frowned at the request. "The granting of a favour is a Legion custom, but even that has limits. I don't think Commandant Eckles would approve. However, I will honour your request. Come tonight at midnight to the treasury." He cast a quick glance to where Captain Jana was replacing the lances in their rack, then lowered his voice, adding, "But don't be seen."

● ● ●

At a few minutes before twelve, Jack and his friends sneaked past the Legion's dormitories. Most of the torches on the walls were extinguished, casting the corridors in an eerie blue-grey glow. Their footsteps shuffled on the uneven flagstones and their breath made clouds in the chill air of Mount Razor.

"At least Hero Academy has central heating," grumbled Danny.

Jack wasn't cold himself, but as he crept on, a shiver passed down his spine. He glanced over his shoulder. He kept expecting a robed figure to appear in the shadows, just like the one that had stolen the second Orb of Foresight. Raina was a shape-shifter, and Jack knew there was a chance she was lurking in disguise at Mount Razor, spying under their noses. It would explain how she knew where to find the Orbs of Foresight in the first place. *We can't trust anyone any more*, Jack thought.

They reached the steep steps to the treasury, where Matthias and a fellow student stood holding pikes. They crossed their weapons as Jack and his friends approached, and the girl with Matthias called, "Who's there?"

"It's all right," said Matthias, as Jack stepped into the torchlight. "They're the friends I mentioned." He took the torch from the wall and led them into a low chamber. In a shallow alcove, the remaining Orb of Foresight rested on a wooden plinth. It glowed with a soft yellow light.

"Go on — touch it," said Ruby.

Before Jack stepped up to the plinth, he slipped the silver spear-baton from his belt and offered it to

Matthias. "To say thank you," he said.

Matthias's eyes widened at the gift, and he reached out, only to draw back his hand. "Thank you, Jack, but I can't. Here in the Legion, weapons are earned through victory in battle. Now, be quick. If you're discovered, we're all in trouble."

Jack cleared his mind, reaching out for the Orb. *Tell me where Raina will strike next*, he willed. *Where is she?*

He closed his eyes and let his fingers fall on the Orb's cold surface. At once, he saw mountains, silhouetted against a stormy sky. The peaks were impossibly steep and jagged, and from their midst he saw a yellow glimmer.

Suddenly, the vision zoomed in so fast he could feel the rush of wind on his face. The yellow light beckoned him closer and closer, until he saw a figure standing on a mountain ledge. The light was a single yellow eye — the stolen Orb of Foresight — within a hooded face, and he knew at once that it was their deadly enemy.

Jack's blood turned to ice, and he wanted to look away. But the yellow stone held him.

He cried out, and suddenly he was back in the chamber with his friends. Sweat slicked his skin, but he had goose pimples too.

"What did you see?" asked Ruby.

"Was it Raina?" added Danny.

Jack took a moment to gain his senses, then nodded his head grimly.

"She's expecting us," he whispered.

CHAPTER 2

THE CLAW MOUNTAINS

JUST BEFORE dawn, Jack and his friends crept into the stables. The air was filled with the earthy smell of the accifaxes.

Flinta seemed to sense their worry, tossing her eagle head and stamping the floor of the stables as Jack tried to fasten the saddle harness.

"You're sure she can support all of us?" said Danny.

"We'll take it slowly," said Jack, climbing on. Ruby came next, sitting behind him.

"If she doesn't like it, she'll let us know," she said.

"That's what I'm worried about," muttered Danny, pulling himself on to the accifax's back awkwardly. The creature snorted. "You know animals and I don't get on. Budge up, will you?"

The three of them were a tight fit on Flinta's back. The accifax huffed a bit at first, but some calming words of encouragement from Jack soon set her at ease. When she trotted from the stable, she did so eagerly.

There were several paths leading down the slopes of Mount Razor. They found the narrowest one, heading roughly north. It was little more than a mountain goat trail across scrubby, scree-strewn land. Danny grumbled from the back of the saddle, worried he was going to fall off, but Jack settled into the accifax's rocking rhythm.

The sun hadn't yet risen in the east, but the upper reaches of the sky were tinged with pink. They hadn't told anyone that they were leaving, not even Commandant Eckles. Jack knew she would never permit them to go and face Raina alone. And if Raina was already lurking in disguise at Mount Razor, the fewer people knew of their mission, the better.

"Are you sure this is the way?" asked Ruby.

Jack stared up at the silhouetted range ahead. There was no doubt it was the same as in his vision. *The Claw Mountains.*

"One hundred per cent," he said. "That's where we'll find Raina."

Soon Mount Razor's fortifications

were way behind them as they crossed the rolling foothills toward the Claw Mountains. The nearer they got, the higher the jagged peaks loomed. Jack wondered how long it would be until they were missed at the school.

"Show me a map, Hawk," said Jack.

His Oracle buzzed in his ear in response. *"Of course, Jack."*

Hawk extended a visor and a holographic display flickered into life just in front of Jack's eyes. It showed a three-dimensional view of the geography. Their location was shown as a blue dot.

"Show Legion outposts," Jack said. "We need to stay clear if we can."

A number of red dots were scattered across the landscape, more than Jack had expected.

"Oh," he said. "Can you plot a safe route, Hawk?"

"Calibrating," said Hawk. A blue line zigzagged through the terrain, and Jack saw that it avoided the outposts, though they'd still pass close to one called Fort Stonetree that sat near the edge of what looked like a huge lake. He asked Hawk to sync with the others, and their Oracles displayed the same image.

"The Summer Sea," said Ruby, reading the name of the large body of water. "Sounds kind of nice."

"The Summer Sea flows from a natural spring in the Claw Mountains," said

Hawk. *"The water temperature remains at a stable twenty-four degrees all year round. The pH is 7.4, with traces of magnesium, sodium ..."*

"That's probably enough information," said Jack, grinning. "We won't be swimming or drinking it." Hawk knew a great deal about many things, but sometimes didn't know when enough was enough. "Will the outpost be heavily guarded, though?"

"My databank says the Fort houses the Hightower Legion's archives and also lists a garrison of twenty Legionaries. They are tasked with protecting the rare Feathered Serpents

that nest beside the lake."

"Feathered Serpents?" said Danny, uneasily.

"I doubt we'll have much time to stick around," said Ruby. "If we come across any Legionaries, let's just pretend we're students on a training exercise."

As they rode on, following Hawk's route, the ground became rougher, with scrubby grass and fallen boulders. The mountains ahead, a silhouette one moment, came alive with colour as the sun crept over the peaks. They were about half a kilometre from the Summer Sea when

Danny said, "Wait, I hear something!"

Jack reined in Flinta, and squinted ahead. He couldn't see anything, but he knew that Danny's ears were a lot better than his eyes, and he trusted his friend. He twisted and saw Danny had taken off his helmet and was turning his head slowly. His ear-tips twitched a little, then he pointed slightly off to the right. "It's coming from that way. People — at least a dozen, I think."

"Maybe we should re-route," said Ruby.

As soon as the words left her mouth, a man crested the low brow of a hill, exactly in line with Danny's finger. He was followed by several others, who walked in marching formation, four abreast, behind him.

"Too late," said Jack. "Danny, put on your helmet."

Jack had given Danny his jousting helmet, in case they needed to disguise his friend's pointed bat-like ears. Danny jammed it on his head. "Weapons in the saddlebags and out of sight," said Jack. "We might be able to talk our way out of this."

As the figure drew nearer, Jack saw it was a man. Like the others he wore full armour and a cloak that brushed the ground. Each member of the guard wore a breastplate emblazoned with a rearing white horse.

"Identify yourselves at once," he called from twenty paces away. Jack saw that the man's hand was on his sword hilt already.

"We're students from Mount Razor, and our mount is thirsty," said Jack. He shifted on Flinta's back to make sure the man could see the Legion sigil on his armour. "We were heading for the Summer Sea to find her water."

The soldier seemed to relax a little, and released his grip on his sword.

"Forgive us," he said. "Times are

troubled of late, and we must remain

on our guard." He pointed south.

"Take a straight line that way and

you will reach a river in under an

hour. The waters of the Summer Sea will not be good for your accifax."

Jack breathed a sigh of relief. It might take them longer than they'd planned to reach the Claw Mountains, but at least their secret was intact. He thanked the soldier and gave Flinta's reins a tug to turn her.

The accifax jerked around, obviously quicker than Danny had expected. Jack heard his friend yelp and then turned to see Danny fall from the saddle and hit the ground hard. As he did, his helmet rolled off through the dust, revealing his strange ears.

"Those ears!" roared the lead soldier. "What is this? Who are you? You're not from Mount Razor! Surround them!" Jack heard the snick of steel as swords were drawn.

With well-drilled precision, the Legionary force spread out in a large circle, weapons bristling inwards.

"I can explain!" said Jack. "We're not your enemy!'"

"The time for explanations is past," said the soldier. "Sentries, attack!"

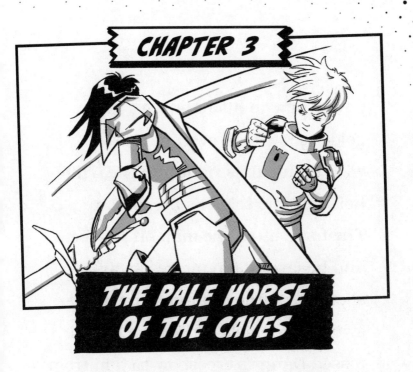

CHAPTER 3

THE PALE HORSE OF THE CAVES

JACK BARELY managed to climb down from the accifax before the first sentry reached him. He didn't have time to draw Blaze, his sunsteel sword, from the saddlebag, so he dodged a downward swipe by side-stepping. He spun, and then let the power flow to his hands. As the golden glow took over, he shoved with both palms right into the white horse on the soldier's breastplate. The force lifted the man off his feet and he landed ten metres away, sliding over the ground. Ruby had swung her shield off her back, and tossed Danny's crossbow to him from Flinta's pack.

"We don't want to fight you!" said Jack, as the sentry climbed to his feet, glowering through the open visor of his helmet.

"Too late!" replied a woman, lifting her sword and charging with a roar.

A beam of fire sliced through the air, melting the ground right in front of her feet. She skidded to a halt. Jack turned and saw Ruby's eyes aglow. The soldier backed away.

"We told you, we're from Mount Razor," said Ruby.

"Lies," said the leader. "You're no Legionaries."

"With powers like that, they can only be Raina's servants," said another soldier. "Kill them!"

Four soldiers rushed at once towards Danny. Jack knew his friend would never use the crossbow on innocents, and sure enough, Danny let it drop. Instead, with the soldiers closing in, he opened his mouth, and

let out a piercing shriek that echoed through the hills. The attackers fell back as if hit by a physical blow, hands clutched over their ears.

"Sorcery!" cried one.

"Jack, look out!" Ruby cried.

Jack spun around just as a soldier with a lance stabbed it towards his chest. He caught the point and twisted, snapping the shaft easily. Then he delivered one of the front kicks he'd learned from Captain Jana in combat training. It connected with the soldier's chin, knocking him out cold.

The rest of the soldiers charged at him. *Too many ... thought Jack. I can't fight them all!*

"Wait!" bellowed the leader.

The soldiers stopped in their tracks, looking confused, with weapons raised and ready.

"Where did you learn to kick like that?" said the leader.

Jack, breathing hard, said, "I said, we've been training at Mount Razor."

The leader smiled for the first time, and waved his hand. "The rest of you, stand down. He is telling the truth — these kids have trained under Captain Jana."

They obeyed at once. The leader came forward and held out a hand, which Jack shook uncertainly. "You know Captain Jana?" he said.

"I was her pupil at Mount Razor," said the leader. "My name is Lieutenant Derik, and I'd recognise her technique anywhere."

"So tell us," said the woman. "What are you really doing here?"

Jack glanced quickly at his friends.

We don't want this getting back to Mount Razor.

"We're on a secret mission in the Claw Mountains," he said. "Sent by Commandant Eckles."

The lieutenant bowed. "Then we will aid you in any way we can," he said. "Come, let us escort you back to our village. It isn't far."

They continued on foot, with Ruby leading Flinta by the reins while Jack walked alongside Derik.

"I offer you our apologies," said the leader. "With Raina's return, we have been on high alert for anything odd. And those ears are very odd indeed."

"Charming," muttered Danny.

"We're from Hero Academy," Jack explained. "We were doing some training exercises at Mount Razor when Raina returned."

Derik arched an eyebrow. "I remember my own training at Mount Razor. I used to go to bed covered in bruises every night! Many of them delivered by Jana herself!"

As they topped the brow of the hill a village came into view below. Its pretty houses, log cabins large and small, littered a green valley surrounded by the Claw Mountains. Sheep and cattle grazed in fenced-off pastures, and on the opposite slope fields of crops were being tended.

"Welcome to Bernshoff," said Derik, as they descended the slope.

They passed under a large wooden gate, painted with the sigil of a white horse. "What's that?" asked Danny.

"That is Porphus, the ghost stallion of the caverns," said Derik. "One thousand years ago, Raina captured him and turned his pure heart evil. But he was freed from this foul corruption when Wulfstan finally defeated Raina. Porphus is a gentle spirit who usually keeps to the caves in the Claw Mountains, though sometimes he has been known to roam the countryside. The children of the village leave hay for him on their windowsills — he's supposed to bring good luck."

Jack felt a sudden chill, and he remembered an image from one of the tapestries in the jousting hall. Raina on a rearing black horse of smoke.

"I think I know why Raina is here," he said. "She wants to capture Porphus again!"

"How far are these caves?" Ruby asked urgently.

"Oh, not far from the village," said the lieutenant. "The springs flow from there into the Summer Sea on the other side of Bernshoff. Wouldn't you like to rest with us a while, though? We have milk, and roasted meats — and fruit juicier than any of the fare you will find at Mount Razor."

"Sounds great!" said Danny. "Lead the—"

"Perhaps later," said Jack. "If you wouldn't mind watering Flinta here, that would be much appreciated, but we'll head to the caves."

"As you wish," said Derik. "Simply follow the high road from the other side of the village and you cannot miss the caves. Be careful inside, though — the place is a warren that spans the entire mountain range and it's easy to get lost."

Jack and his friends left Flinta with a stable lad. Derik was right — the route was clear, and it wasn't long before they saw several dark openings in the mountainside ahead, several belching wisps of steam.

"Do you think Raina will come here?" asked Ruby.

Jack shrugged. "Dunno. Just remember she can change her shape. If we see anyone at all, we have to be suspicious."

They edged inside the largest of

the caves. The air was humid, with bubbling pools dotted across the floor. Water dripped from the roof.

"Hawk, do you have a map of the cave system?" asked Jack.

"Negative," replied his Oracle. *"They haven't been properly explored. If I had to theorise, I would assume the tunnels and caves were formed by the movement of ancient magma channels. Clearly the water from the springs is heated by underground deposits of molten rock."*

As they delved deeper, the steam dampened Jack's clothing under his armour. Hawk automatically activated a bright torch on the Oracle earpiece. Danny and Ruby's Oracles did the same. Three arcs of light lit up the dark rock passage ahead.

"I really don't want to get lost," whispered Danny. "This place gives me the creeps."

Soon the tunnel opened out further, and ahead Jack heard splashing. They found themselves looking down into a vast cavern filled with a bright green pool. A magnificent horse with a flowing white mane stood in the shallows, drinking.

"It's him!" whispered Ruby. "Porphus!"

Danny's foot scuffed the ground and sent a scatter of rocks tumbling from where they stood into the pool below.

The mighty horse looked up, startled, then gave a whinny that echoed through the cavern. Jack saw that his body wasn't entirely solid, but seemed to blur at the edges as he moved.

"Easy," said Jack, fearing the ghost stallion might be about to bolt.

The horse tossed his mane, then trotted through the water, barely disturbing the surface.

"He's beautiful," said Ruby, as she began to clamber down a steep bank towards to the pool's edge. "Let's take a closer look."

"Er, are you sure?" said Danny. "Don't horses bite?"

Jack gave him a friendly slap on the shoulder. "Come on — he's friendly, remember?"

Danny, still grumbling under his breath, followed him down the slope.

At the water, Jack stooped and dipped his hand in. It was as warm as a bath, and almost silky to touch. "I wish I'd brought my swimming things," he said with a smile.

Ruby was holding out a hand to Porphus, and the horse approached with his head bowed. Up close, Jack realised he wasn't a ghost at all. His body seemed to be made of dense steam, neither solid nor transparent.

"We can't let Raina turn him into a monster," said Ruby, letting her hand stroke the stallion's nose. Jack saw her fingers become moist at the touch of the steam.

"Agreed," said Jack.

"So what are we going to do?" asked Danny.

Porphus turned his head and approached him, causing Danny to trip and land in the water. The ghost stallion came up and nuzzled his neck. "He likes you," said Ruby.

"Or he's trying to eat me," said Danny, but his lips curled into the beginnings of a smile.

Jack looked back to the tunnel. The caverns were tight and twisting and not at all the kind of place he wanted to be trapped in with Raina. *I'm sure she's on her way, but we don't need to just wait around for her to attack us.*

"I say we set up an ambush," he said. "If Raina thinks she can just come and claim Porphus, she doesn't know a thing about Team Hero!"

CHAPTER 4

RAINA ATTACKS

JACK'S BREATH formed clouds in the air and his hands glowed gold as he heaved the final wooden log into place. A starlit night had fallen, and there was still no sign of their enemy.

"Nice work!" said Ruby, stepping back to examine the makeshift defence. Ten logs, all sharpened into spikes, bristled from the cave mouth leading into the mountain.

But will it stop Raina?

"Where's Danny?" asked Jack.

"Still petting Porphus," said Ruby. "I think he really likes him, despite all the grumbling."

"I heard that!" Danny called back. "Super-hearing, remember?"

Jack smiled — It was good to have a joke when everything else seemed so serious. He peered through a gap in the stockade. "Hawk, give me night-vision, please."

His Oracle obeyed at once, extending a visor over Jack's face.

The landscape showed in various shades of black and green. Down in the valley, firelight shone through the windows of the pretty houses in Bernshoff, but the streets were deserted. Derik and his sentries were enforcing a curfew to keep people out of harm's way.

The village is probably safe, thought Jack. *It's what's behind us that Raina really wants.*

Danny's footsteps made him turn. His friend wiped a sleeve across his sweating brow. "It's so hot down there. I feel like a boiled egg."

"How's Porphus?" asked Ruby.

Danny's face lit up in a wide smile. "Oh, he's great ... I mean — fine. He's fine. Just a horse, you know." Ruby laughed, but then Danny's smile evaporated. "Someone's coming," he said.

Jack looked out from the stockade of spikes again, but couldn't see anything. "Are you sure?" he asked.

Danny cupped his hands around his large ears. Their tips twitched, then he nodded. "Certain."

Seeing the glistening sweat on his friend's face gave Jack an idea. "Hawk, can you switch to thermal imaging, please."

The greens of the world changed
to warmer colours. The mountains
beyond were all black, cold stone,
but the village below had areas of
orange and yellow. *There!* A red figure
in a dark hooded cloak was moving
at speed around the outskirts, then
straight along the path towards them.
He was sure it was the same person
he'd seen when he touched the Orb of
Foresight.

"Raina!" said Jack. "It has to be.
Activate your thermal visors!"

The red figure was closing in
fast, slipping between boulders in
darting runs.

"I've got this!" said Ruby, her eyes already starting to glow.

"Wait!" said Jack.

But she'd already rounded the stockade and crouched. Twin fire-beams shot from her eyes at the approaching target, so bright Jack had to rip the visor from his face. In the firelight, he saw Raina spread her hands. She wore a pair of bright steel gauntlets. As soon as the flames struck, they rebounded straight towards Ruby.

Jack threw himself at his friend, barrelling her out of the way. A flash of fire and light exploded behind him, showering them both with ash and splintered wood. Jack turned back to the see the stockade was smashed to charred pieces.

Danny!

There was no sign of his friend, but he'd been standing right there, not five seconds before.

Jack looked to where Raina stood. *It's almost like she knew exactly what Ruby would do ...*

Jack helped Ruby to her feet.

"How can I fight her if she just deflects my fire back at me?" she asked.

"Let me!" said Jack. "You find Danny!"

He charged at Raina, drawing Blaze

as he ran. His enemy didn't move, but spread her arms and waited.

He swung the blade at her neck, but she ducked and slid away, as smooth as water. Jack's weight and the

momentum of the sword carried him stumbling past. He fell to his knees, springing up quickly to twist and face her. Raina stood perfectly still and untroubled.

"I expected more," she said.

Jack couldn't see her face underneath her hood, but he heard the smile in her tone. *She's quick, but she can't face two attacks at once.*

He flung Blaze at her, and the blade spun through the air. As she slipped aside to dodge the sword, Jack rushed her and clamped his arms around her body. An earthy smell filled his nostrils as she screeched to get free.

Beneath the cloak he felt hard bone, and her shriek cut through his brain like a knife. Hands clawed at his face, nails raking at his eyes. He let go.

Raina pounced into the air, a leaping shadow, and landed on the other side of the smashed stockade. "Eckles is correct that you share Gore's power of super-strength," she said. "But you'll never be as great as him!"

And then she was gone, disappearing into darkness. Danny stumbled to Jack's side, supported by Ruby. The shoulder of his tunic was torn, his hair was dishevelled and one side of his face was covered in ash. He must have been blasted back by the exploding stockade, but he seemed unhurt.

"We need to get after her," said Jack.

Ruby nodded, but Danny was frowning. "Why did she say you shared Gore's power? After you won at jousting, Commandant Eckles said you shared *Wulfstan's* power."

"You're right," said Jack. "That's weird.'"

"Hang on," said Ruby. "How does Raina know what Eckles said at all?"

Jack's blood ran cold. *It can mean only one thing.* "She must have been there during the jousting contest. *In* the school." *Just as I feared.*

There was no time to worry about that now. The three friends charged over the smouldering logs and into the caverns. Danny strung a shaft on his energy bow, and Ruby held her mirrored shield ready.

"Where did you leave Porphus?" Jack whispered.

"By the pool," said Danny, leading them down the forked passage. More tunnels branched off on every side.

"Careful," said Ruby. "Raina could be hiding anywhere!"

But when they reached the cavern, Jack was horrified to see Raina wasn't hiding at all. She stood on the banks of the pool, hands reaching out to Porphus.

"Come to me, old friend," she hissed. The horse tossed its mane, and stamped a forehoof. He seemed unwilling.

"Leave him alone!' shouted Danny. "If you hurt him, I'll—"

"You'll do nothing," said Raina, then turned back to the horse. As she did so, a single glowing light shone from under her hood.

The missing Orb of Foresight!

Jack watched aghast as Porphus's own eyes began to glow a sinister shade of blue. He seemed to calm at once, and took a tentative step towards the sorceress. The steam of the stallion's body thickened and darkened into swirls of black smoke, rippling with muscle.

"What's happening to him?" said Danny in despair.

"He's bewitched," murmured Jack.

Jack could only look on in horror as Porphus transformed into something demonic, his ears lengthening and sharpening into hooked horns, and claws sprouting from his hooves. Raina gripped his mane and flung a leg over his back. She patted Porphus's neck, and her steed rose up for a moment on his hind legs then splashed down into the water. Porphus opened his mouth and blue flame flickered through his teeth.

"After all these centuries, we are finally united, my steed," cried Raina. "No one will stop us now!"

CHAPTER 5

REIGN OF FIRE

PORPHUS BLASTED a snort of flame
from his nostrils, and the pool around
his feet began to steam and bubble
as it heated up with strange, blue
energy. Jack heard Hawk's voice, calm
in his ear.

*"The cave temperature is rising at an
alarming rate."*

"Thanks for telling me," said Jack, wiping the sweat from his brow.

"What do we do?" asked Ruby.

"We need to get Raina off that horse!" said Danny. He lined up his crossbow and fired. The bolt sang through the air, but Raina held up a hand and the bolt bounced off her gauntlet, fizzing into the water.

"It will take more than your Team Hero toys to defeat me," she said. "I've killed more of your number than you could ever count."

Ruby's eyes began to glow, but Jack reached for her. "Don't!" he said. "You might harm Porphus."

Raina urged the stallion from the water. "My reign of fire begins now," she said. "And it will not end until Mount Razor is rubble and the Legion crawls to me on its knees. Come, my steed, let us wake the mountain and shatter this place into ruins!"

She drove her heels into Porphus's flanks and the horse surged upwards in an impossible leap. Jack had no choice but to dive aside, shoving Danny the other way. As Porphus galloped past them, his glowing blue clawed hooves gouged splinters from the rock, and Jack felt a searing heat on his face. Then Raina and her mount were gone, heading back down the tunnel towards the cave mouth.

"Do you think they're heading to Mount Razor?" said Danny. "We have to get word to Commandant Eckles to prepare the defences."

"Owl," said Ruby to her Oracle. "Send a distress signal." A moment later, she frowned and shook her head. "We're too deep underground. We have to get out of the caves."

The three of them ran after Raina, stumbling half-blind through the ash.

But when they reached the cave mouth, the steam had cleared and there was no sign of Raina or her mount. The lights of Bernshoff twinkled below. "I don't think she came this way," Jack said.

"Then what's she planning?" asked Danny.

The sound of hooves made them all spin around. "Huh?" said Jack.

Back in the warren of caves, he saw a stream of blue fire whipping past, then disappearing down another tunnel. "She's still in there!" he said.

At the same moment, the ground beneath his feet began to tremble.

"I think I know what 'wake the mountain' means," said Ruby. "She's causing an earthquake!"

The floor of the cave mouth split apart, and an unnatural bright-blue glow appeared in the crack.

"Worse!" said Jack, staring at his friends. The blue light bathed their terrified faces. "This isn't just a

mountain — it's a volcano!'

Porphus charged past again, even faster, and on his back Raina cackled.

"She's running in circles through the tunnels," said Danny. "Porphus's energy is affecting the magma! They're going to destroy this whole place!"

Jack glanced again at the village below the mountain. An eruption would completely destroy it.

Rocks began to fall from above and the ground shifted so much he almost lost his footing. "The sentries need to evacuate Bernshoff!" he said. "You guys — find Derik, and quickly."

"What about you?" asked Ruby.

Jack pointed back into the caves. "I'll stop her if I can."

"How?" said Danny. "You can't stop a speeding horse on your own!"

"I won't be on my own," said Jack. He gave a whistle.

After a few seconds, Flinta came bounding along the path from the village, the breeze ruffling her mane. She halted in front of them, her black eyes focused on Jack and her furred flanks heaving.

"Go!" said Jack. "We need to get

everyone out of Bernshoff. If I fail, the village will be decimated."

Ruby nodded grimly. "Then don't fail."

Jack bumped fists with his friends then sprinted downhill towards the village. Steadying himself on the shifting ground, Jack gripped the accifax's reins and mounted the animal. He gazed into the bright blue glowing cave. Sinister light was streaming through the cracks already.

"It's down to us," he said to Flinta. "Are you ready, girl?"

The accifax lifted her eagle head and let out a defiant squawk. Then she launched herself into the cauldron.

CHAPTER 6

THE FACE OF THE ENEMY

JACK READIED himself at the junction of tunnels where Raina had last appeared. He drew his silver baton from the holster in his belt, and pressed the switch to extend it to full length. He tried to remember Captain Jana's instructions from back at Mount Razor, and tucked the spear tightly under his arm and over his hip. Then he tugged Flinta's reins and thundered into the tunnel. He knew that Raina would be riding Porphus in the opposite direction, and it would be only seconds until he met her head on.

"Yah!" Jack powered Flinta onward. Around him, the walls cracked apart, shooting jets of blue light across his path. Then a shape appeared ahead, coming impossibly fast. Jack barely had time to steady his spear before Raina shot past, howling manically. Flinta shrieked in pain as Porphus's flaming breath scorched her feathers. Jack found himself hurtling through the horse's smoke trails, and Flinta came to a juddering halt.

The rocks of the tunnel walls seemed to be mutating in the supernatural blue energy, and each breath felt like it was poisoning the inside of his throat.

"The energy forces here are interfering with my reception," said Hawk. *"I recommend moving to a safer location."*

"Not yet," said Jack. *I just need to be quicker next time*, he thought.

If there *was* a next time. The mountain felt ready to blow at any second.

Flinta's eagle eyes bulged in panic, and Jack lay down close to her feathered head. "We can do this," he said. "Be brave."

The accifax cawed gently in response and picked up speed again down the tunnel. Jack felt his strength surge into his hands, one gripping the reins and the other clasped tight over his spear. As they rounded a bend, Porphus and his rider appeared once more. In the darkness, all Jack saw was a flaming horse's head and the single yellow glow of the Orb of Foresight that Raina used as her eye.

You're not getting past me again! He levelled the spear-tip at the place he knew Raina's body would be.

They galloped full tilt right at one another, and kept Flinta on a straight course at his enemy. The tunnel was disintegrating all around, the walls crumbling inwards in a haze of blue light. At the last second, he felt the spear-tip connect. Raina's scream pierced the crash of rock and the ring of electricity.

SMASH!

A brute force lifted Jack from the saddle. He heard Porphus's snort and Flinta's shrieking cry, then his body slammed into rock. He felt himself rolling, further than he thought possible. The pain was everywhere, and

he threw up his hands to protect his head. Then he plunged into water.

All he could see through the darkness was bubbles. Twisting his body around, he followed them upwards, bursting up through the surface. He was alive, somehow, but the danger wasn't past. Rocks tumbled into the water, and he realised the tunnels must have collapsed, depositing him in some sort of underground river. The water churned in white tips all around him, and he saw Flinta's clawed legs scrabbling upside-down, then a sodden flank, then a saddle.

There was no sign of Raina or Porphus.

Jack took a deep breath as the water swallowed him again. The torrent gripped his body and dragged him downstream. He tried to reach for

Flinta's reins, but the accifax swept past helplessly. He felt the rocky walls and tried to grab them but his fingers just slipped past.

But as his head broke into the air again, he was dimly aware of light ahead — natural light.

Suddenly, Jack's stomach dropped away, and he plummeted over a rocky shelf, limbs flailing. He plunged back under, this time into what felt like calmer water. He had no time to draw a breath, and panicked as another current pulled him deeper into darkness. He kicked against it, striving for the natural light above. His hands glowed like golden beacons as he clawed his way up the rocks with powerful strokes.

Got to make it ...

He couldn't hold on much longer. He had to breathe, and when he did the water would flood his lungs and it would all be over.

With a huge, final heave, he pulled himself in the direction of the surface. *Too far ...*

Against his will, his mouth opened, and he gasped in not water, but air.

Fresh, sweet air!

He looked up at a raging waterfall cascading from the mountainside.

I just fell down that!

Beams of blue light drifted across the sky above, and he was treading water near the shore of a vast, steaming lake. *The Summer Sea!* Flinta was already dragging herself on to the bank. She shook her fur, throwing off spray. She turned to Jack and opened her beak in a squawk. Several armoured figures were rushing along the banks, and Jack recognised Ruby and Danny among them. He swam over, and soon his feet found the lake bed. He had just staggered out when he saw another shape bobbing in the shallows — a black-cloaked figure floating face-down.

"Raina," he mumbled. She must have fallen into the spring and been flushed out too.

Cautiously he waded over, gripped the limp body, then dragged it with him to dry land. He rolled the figure over on to her back just as his friends arrived with Derik and the other sentries from Bernshoff.

"Is she dead?" asked Ruby.

Jack carefully pulled back the edge of her hood.

The face that looked back at him was one he knew well.

"Captain Jana!" he said. Behind him, he heard Derik suck in a breath.

The blind warrior wasn't wearing her glasses any more. One eye was closed, and where the other should be, was the missing Orb of Foresight.

As the waves of shock passed, Jack slowly began to understand. Raina was a shape-shifter, and as they suspected, she'd been watching them all along, from the first day they arrived at Mount Razor. He thought back to all the conversations he'd had with Captain Jana, the secrets and tactics they'd shared. By all accounts, she'd been teaching at the school for years!

"Raina was more devious than we ever imagined," said Derik. "She's

been fooling the entire Legion. Even
Commandant Eckles!"

Jack was about to feel for a pulse on
Raina's neck, when her hand shot up
and struck him hard across the cheek.
Through the white flash of pain, he
saw her leap up.

"Fools!" she said. "You think a little water can kill me?"

The sentries drew their weapons, as did Danny. Ruby's eyes shone with fire.

Jack shook his head to clear it and slid Blaze from its sheath. "There's nowhere to run," he said. "It's over."

Raina's face shifted, becoming thinner, with higher cheekbones and marble-smooth skin. Her mouth twisted into a grin, revealing lines of blackened, sharp teeth. A forked tongue parted her lips. Only the Orb of Foresight remained the same, gleaming in its socket. *Is this her true form?* Jack wondered.

"You're wrong," she said. "This war has only just begun."

"Look out!" roared Derik, pointing at the lake.

There, at the top of the waterfall, somehow standing steady in the torrent, was Porphus. He leapt, sailing in a great smoking arc through the air. They all watched, aghast, as he thumped down into the mud nearby. Raina shot across the shore and pounced on to the stallion's back.

Jack heard the

twang of bowstrings as arrows flew through the air, but Raina was already galloping away. They disappeared over a ridge, leaving a wake of smoking, scorched earth behind. "Something tells me that she'll return soon enough," said Jack.

He looked back at the mountain. A few small fissures had opened, and bright blue lava flowed sluggishly down the mountainside. But it looked like they'd prevented the eruption and the village of Bernshoff would be safe.

"We need to alert Mount Razor," he said. "The Legion needs to be informed what we're dealing with."

"You think we can defeat her?" asked Ruby.

Jack looked at his friends. Raina was unlike any foe they'd faced before. Not even Wulfstan Hightower himself had fully finished her off.

He clenched his fists until they glowed gold. "We're Team Hero," he said. "We'll never stop trying."

THE END

ADAM BLADE

TEAM HERO

ARMY OF DARKNESS

MEGA-SELLING
AUTHOR OF
Beast
Quest

READ ON FOR A SNEAK
PEEK AT BOOK 11:

RMY of DARKNES

CHAPTER 1

WULFSTAN'S CACHE

JACK PEERED through one of the archive's narrow windows. Outside, the Summer Sea sparkled beneath snow-capped mountain peaks. Steam wafted up from the clear water.

Jack rubbed his injured arm, as Ruby appeared at his side. "Still sore?" she asked.

Jack grimaced. "Raina almost dislocated my shoulder while we were jousting."

Danny looked up from under his fringe of black hair. "You gave as good as you got," he said. "Raina will need time to recover."

"I wonder where she holed up for the night," Jack murmured. He, Ruby, and Danny had rested here at Fort Stonetree, after fighting Raina the Vile, an evil shape-shifter. The battle hadn't been easy, but they'd revealed her disguise as Captain Jana, the much-respected Legion combat instructor at Mount Razor. And while they hadn't been able to stop Raina from regaining control of her steed, Porphus, the ghost stallion, at least they'd prevented her from erupting a volcano onto the town of Bernshoff. They'd defeated her.

For now...

In the cold light of morning, as Jack stared out at the still-smouldering mountains near Bernshoff, the victory seemed bittersweet. Reunited with her smoke steed, Raina was more powerful than ever.

Ruby picked up Jack's thought.

Check out the next book:
ARMY OF DARKNESS
to find out what happens next!

IN EVERY BOOK OF
TEAM HERO SERIES
ONE there is a special
Power Token. Collect
all four tokens to get
an exclusive Team Hero
Club pack. The pack
contains everything you and
your friends need to form your
very own Team Hero Club.

MEMBERSHIP CARDS · MEMBERSHIP CERTIFICATE · STICKERS · POWER GAME · BOOKMARKS

Just fill in the form below, send it in with your four tokens
and we'll send you your Team Hero Club Pack.

SEND TO: Team Hero Club Pack Offer, Hachette Children's Books,
Marketing Department, Carmelite House, 50 Victoria Embankment,
London, EC4Y 0DZ.

CLOSING DATE: 31st December 2018

WWW.TEAMHEROBOOKS.CO.UK

Please complete using capital letters *(UK and Republic of Ireland residents only)*

FIRST NAME

SURNAME

DATE OF BIRTH

ADDRESS LINE 1

ADDRESS LINE 2

ADDRESS LINE 3

POSTCODE

PARENT OR GUARDIAN'S EMAIL

I'd like to receive Team Hero email newsletters and information about
other great Hachette Children's Group offers (I can unsubscribe at any time)

*Terms and conditions apply. For full terms and conditions please go to
teamherobooks.co.uk/terms*

*TEAM HERO Club packs
available while stocks last.
Terms and conditions apply.*

COLLECT ALL OF SERIES THREE!

**TEAM HERO
BOOK 1
OUT NOW!**